The Adventures of Goliath

Goliath and the
Cub Scouts

The Adventures of
Goliath

Goliath and the
Cub Scouts

Terrance Dicks

Illustrated by
Valerie Littlewood

BARRON'S
New York

First edition for the United States and the Philippines
published 1990 by Barron's Educational Series, Inc.

First published 1989 by Piccadilly Press Ltd., London, England

All inquiries should be addressed to:
Barron's Educational Series, Inc.
250 Wireless Boulevard
Hauppauge, New York 11788

International Standard Book No. 0-8120-4493-2

Library of Congress Catalog Card No. 90-3392

Library of Congress Cataloging-in-Publication Data

Dicks, Terrance.
    Goliath and the Cub Scouts / Terrance Dicks; illustrated by Valerie
Littlewood.
        p.   cm. — (The Adventures of David and Goliath)
    Summary: Canine Goliath helps David find a most unusual thief who
committed an "impossible crime" by removing a valuable trophy from a
locked room.
    ISBN-0-8120-4493-2
    [1. Dogs—Fiction. 2. Mystery and detective stories.] I. Littlewood,
Valerie, ill. II. Title. III. Series: Dicks, Terrance. Adventures of David and
Goliath.
PZ7.D5627Gq   1990
[Fic]—dc 20
                                                    90-33992
                                                        CIP
                                                        AC

CONTENTS

Chapter One

A Crime on Cub Night

William pulled the ends of his scarf through his ring and adjusted it with care. "Well, David, when are you going to join?"

David was sitting cross-legged on the rug, leaning against his dog, Goliath, who was so huge and shaggy that he made a sort of living sofa. "Oh, one day."

William tugged at the ends of the scarf, making sure they were straight.

"Why don't you come tonight, just as

1

a visitor? You can watch what goes on and see if you think you'd like it."

"You don't give up!" said David.

William was one of David's best friends at school. He was an enthusiastic Cub Scout and he'd been trying to persuade David to join for ages.

"I'm just keeping the Cub Scout Law," said William solemnly.

"What law?"

"A Cub Scout always does his best, thinks of others before himself, and does a good deed every day!" William grinned. "I'm doing my best to get you to join. I'm thinking of you, because I know you'll enjoy it, and I'm doing you a favor by getting you to come today instead of putting it off like one of the Banderlog!"

"The who?"

"The Banderlog, they're in the *Jungle*

Book by Rudyard Kipling. The Cub Scouts use lots of names from the *Jungle Book*."

"But who are the Banderlog?" David was still puzzled.

"The Banderlog are the monkey people. They're always chatting about what they're going to do, but they never get anything done."

"All right, you win," said David. "I'd hate to be like one of the Banderlog! Hang on though, what about Goliath?"

The big dog tilted his head at the sound of his name.

"Can't you take him home first?"

David shook his head. "Mom and Dad are out shopping—and it's not a good idea to leave Goliath in the house on his own."

"Why, what does he do?"

"Runs up and down knocking over the furniture, chews up all the carpets, and howls like a werewolf so all the neighbors complain."

"Then he'll just have to come too," said William cheerfully.

A car tooted outside. "Come on, that's my Cub Master."

Grabbing a somewhat weedy looking plant in a pot, William ran from the room, and David and Goliath followed.

Parked outside William's house was a battered old car. A tall, cheerful-looking young man in a beret was at the wheel and crammed into the car itself was an amazing number of Cub Scouts. William ran up to him. "Can I bring a visitor tonight, please?"

"Certainly, the more the merrier. You're the visitor, aren't you, David?"

David nodded. In civilian life he was Mr. Rogers the music teacher and he knew David well.

Suddenly Goliath ran out of the house. He'd been saying goodbye to

William's parents who always fussed over him and gave him treats.

Mr. Rogers had never seen Goliath before and he stared at him in amazement. "Good grief, what's that? A young mammoth?"

"That's Goliath, my dog," said David. "If I'm coming, I'm afraid he's got to come as well."

"Oh well, Cub Scouts are expected to 'Be Prepared'—and I suppose that means being prepared for dogs as big as donkeys. Get in, then—if you can!"

William and David climbed into the already crowded car, hauling Goliath in after them.

"Hold tight!" shouted Mr. Rogers and set off on the short journey to school.

"Nothing to worry about," said William as they drove off. "We're jammed in too tight to fall out!"

William's Cub Scout Pack met in the new school gym. It was a new building, a sort of annex to the school itself. David and Goliath tucked themselves in a quiet corner and watched the meeting begin.

First the Cub Scout Pack formed into dens and gathered around their leader for the opening ceremony, which ended with all the cubs chanting, "We will do our best."

Excited by the noise, Goliath threw back his head and howled. David was very embarrassed but Mr. Rogers only laughed. "The ceremony's called the Grand Howl, he was only joining in! Come and have a doughnut and some orange juice."

David enjoyed the refreshments and so did Goliath. All the Cubs fussed over him and fed him bits of their doughnuts. After the refreshments the serious business of the evening began.

This evening's theme was Crime Prevention, and a young policeman had come from the local police station. He talked to them about the importance of proper locks on doors and windows. "Let's all go outside," he said, "and we'll do a security check on the building."

"Right—line up outside," ordered Mr. Rogers and everyone filed out. Everyone except Goliath. He'd become bored and had gone to sleep, so they left him snoozing in the corner.

They all went outside and walked around the building. The policeman pointed out places where security could be improved and then he left. When they got back to the front of the gym they heard a frantic barking from inside.

"I'm afraid that's Goliath," said David. "He hates being left alone."

Mr. Rogers unlocked the door and Goliath came bounding out, nearly knocking David over in his excitement.

After that two of the dens stayed outside to practice tracking. The other dens went back into the gym to play a noisy game with balloons. Goliath joined in, bursting several balloons in his excitement.

Cubs came up and showed their Master the work they'd been doing to earn points toward their different merit badges.

William only got one point for his potted plant. But he didn't seem too disappointed. "It's nearly time for the Best Den award," he told David afterward. "I think we might win this week—in spite of my poor old plant! I'm the denner, so I'll get to keep the shield for a week—if we win."

"Win what?"

"The den that gets most points over the evening wins a badge with 'Best Den' written on it. This Pack's badge is really special. There's a medal in the

center—and it belonged to B-P himself! Mr. Rogers found it in a junk shop and presented it to the Pack. Actually it's worth a lot of money."

"Who's B-P?"

William looked shocked. "Lord Baden-Powell. He's the man who started the whole Scout and Cub movement."

Their Cub Master called the Pack together and William lined up at attention at the head of his den.

Mr. Rogers looked at his notebook. "This week the winner of the shield and medal is—Den Six!"

David saw William step forward, beaming with pride.

Mr. Rogers reached up to the top shelf of the corner cupboard where the Cub Scouts kept their equipment. "Well done, Den Six! It gives me great pleasure . . ."

He took down the badge and then broke off, staring at it in amazement.

It took David a moment to realize what was wrong. At the center of the shield there was nothing but an empty metal peg.

The medal was gone.

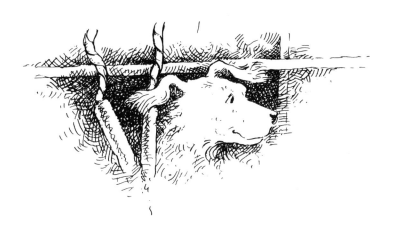

Chapter Two

The Impossible Crime

The whole Pack joined in the hunt for the missing medal. They searched every inch of the gym, but the medal was nowhere to be found.

"Who had it last?" asked David, when they'd all given up.

The denner of Den Five was a serious-looking boy called Peter. "My den won the shield last time so I had it all week.

I handed it to Mr. Rogers at the beginning of the meeting. You lose five points if you don't return it on time!"

"Are you sure the medal was in place when the badge was handed in? Could it have dropped off on the way or something?"

"I know the medal was in place when Peter handed in the badge," said Mr. Rogers. "I remember noticing how it flashed in the sunlight from the window. I put the badge up on the top shelf just as I always do. Now the badge is still here but the medal's gone."

"There *was* a time when the gym was empty," said David. "When we all went outside with the policeman. Someone could have sneaked in and taken the medal then."

"No they couldn't," said the Cub Master.

"When I checked the gym it was

empty, so I closed the door and locked it behind me."

David looked up at an open window high in the roof . . . "Someone could have climbed in through the window while we were all outside."

"No they couldn't," said Peter. "We were all walking around the building with the policeman, remember? I think we'd have noticed if there was a burglar on the roof—and so would the policeman. After that, my den and Den Six stayed outside playing tracking games. We were all around the gym—the place was surrounded."

"And the gym wasn't left empty either," said William. "Goliath was asleep, remember, so we left him inside." He looked at David. "All that barking wasn't just to be let out—he was telling us about the robbery!"

Mr. Rogers looked around. "If anyone

took the medal for some kind of joke, they can own up now and we'll say no more about it."

He waited for a moment, but nobody spoke.

"So, to sum up," he went on, "the medal was in sight of the full Pack nearly all the time. The only time it was left, there was a big dog guarding it, and the building was locked and surrounded, so no one could have got in or out without being seen. If none of you boys took it—and I don't believe you did—what we've got here is an impossible crime!"

After the meeting was over, William and Peter went to David's house with him to talk things over.

Peter was an avid reader of detective stories.

"In a mystery story, it's always the Least Likely Person who committed the crime. All we've got to do is work out who that is!"

They all thought hard.

"You don't mean Mr. Rogers?" said William, shocked.

Peter shook his head. "There's someone even more unlikely."

"Who?"

"The policeman—the one who gave the talk."

"That's the silliest idea I ever heard," said William.

"How do we know he was a real policeman?" demanded Peter. "Anyone can rent a uniform from a costume store."

"What do you think, David?" asked William.

David thought it was a pretty foolish

idea too, but he didn't want to hurt Peter's feelings. "I suppose it's *possible* . . . Why don't we check up on him?"

David led the way to the local police station.

For some reason the station seemed empty when they arrived. There was certainly no one behind the reception counter.

They looked around uneasily, wondering what to do.

"Now what?" asked William.

"Don't worry," said David. "Someone will be out to speak to us soon."

That was where he made his mistake, using the word "speak."

Goliath only knew one or two simple commands—but "Speak!" was one of them. He let out a series of deep

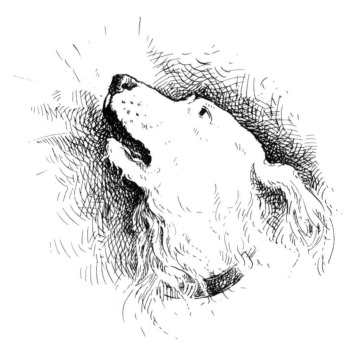

crashing barks that shook the police
station.

There was immediate pandemonium.

All the police dogs started barking in
the kennels behind the station, and
policemen rushed in from all directions.

"What's the matter?" shouted one of

them. "Are we being burglarized?"

"It's all right," said David. "Just a misunderstanding."

The young policeman started making a fuss over Goliath, telling him he'd make a fine police dog.

"If only they knew!" thought David. A big police sergeant appeared from behind the counter, clutching a steaming cup of coffee. He looked at David and Goliath and Peter and William and said, "Now, now, now, what's going on?"

"Sorry about the fuss," said David. "My dog got a bit overexcited. I just wanted to ask a simple question."

"Yes?" said the sergeant suspiciously.

David continued. "Did a policeman give a talk to a Cub Scout Pack earlier this evening?"

"Not as far as I know!"

Peter was listening hard. "Aha!" he said triumphantly.

He took up the questioning himself. "Do you have an Officer . . ." He looked at his notebook. "An Officer Foskett at the station?"

"Never heard of him."

"Maybe we got the name wrong?" suggested William. "Have you got a very tall, young officer here? Reddish brown hair and a beaky nose?"

"No one like that at this station," said the sergeant definitely.

David and William looked at each other in amazement. Could Peter's far-fetched idea really be the right one? Was it possible that the pleasant young policeman had really been a criminal mastermind, cunningly disguised as a policeman in order to steal their precious medal?

No it wasn't.

Another young policeman came forward. "I remember, Sarge. Look, it's in the book here. Visit to Cub Scouts by Crime Prevention Officer. It was all part of the new Community Relations Project."

The sergeant frowned. "First I've heard of it."

"It was all fixed up while you were on leave," said the helpful officer.

"Well, who's this P.C. Foskett, then? There's no one like that here."

"Well," said the policeman patiently, "we were short of bodies, so we got the sixth precinct to lend us young Foskett. He's a new arrival, straight from police college and very enthusiastic about Community Relations."

The sergeant sighed, took a drink of coffee, and looked down at the three boys and the big dog. "Well, there you are then, does that solve your problem?"

"Well, not really," said David. "But at least it answers one question."

"What's all this about then?" asked the sergeant, who was obviously still suspicious. "I hope there's no complaint about this officer? Maybe you'd better come and have a word with the captain . . ."

"No, no, no," said Peter hastily. "There's no need for anything like that. Officer Foskett did a very good job; we were all very pleased."

"So why are you all here asking questions about him?"

"Er, well, er," stammered Peter, and looked desperately at the others.

It was William who came to the rescue. Flourishing his official Cub Scout notebook he said, "It's a sort of project, you see, to earn points for one of our badges. We have to do a report, and part of that is checking up on everything."

It was all a bit vague and unlikely, but luckily it seemed enough to satisfy the sergeant, who really only wanted to get back to his cup of coffee.

"Well, you've got nothing to worry about," said the sergeant. "You've had an official visit from an official policeman, all fair and square."

"Thank you very much, Sergeant. I'm sorry to have taken up your time," said David hastily, and hurried everyone out into the street.

He turned to Peter. "Sorry, Peter, looks like he was a genuine policeman!"

Peter still clung to his theory of the Least Likely Person. "Well, if it wasn't the policeman it *must* be Mr. Rogers. Maybe he's gotten into the clutches of a foreign spy ring, or lost all his money gambling. I'm going to check up on him!"

Peter marched off.

David shook his head. "I reckon all those detective stories have softened his brain!"

William said, "I knew it was an unlikely idea all along! *My* idea's much better."

"What idea?"

"Come around to my house after school tomorrow and I'll tell you," said William, adding mysteriously, "And I'll need your help!"

Chapter Three

William's Plan

When David got to William's house next day he was astonished to find his friend changing into Cub Scout uniform.

"I thought Cubs only met once a week?"

"They do," said William.

David told Goliath to sit and leaned back against him. "All right, William, what's going on?"

"Well, not being a Cub Scout, you

probably don't even realize that there's not one but two Cub Scout Packs in our school!"

"I do actually," said David. "Mr. Rogers was telling me. I imagine so many people wanted to be Cubs they had to start a second pack."

"That's right—and that's us. We're Pack Two. Now the others, Pack One, like to show off a bit. They call themselves the A Team, just because they started first. Really both packs are exactly the same—except for one thing. We've got the B-P medal and they haven't!"

David stared at him. "I can understand they'd feel a bit jealous—but surely they wouldn't . . ."

"I don't think they'd steal it," said William hurriedly. "But they might *borrow* it as a sort of tease, a practical joke. And just think—a Cub, in uniform, could have got in and out of the gym without being noticed!" He looked at David. "Well, what do you think?"

"It's a better idea than Peter's one about the policeman!"

"I'm glad you think so," said William. "Pack One holds their meeting tonight, and I plan to be there. I'm going to need your help—and Goliath's as well!"

Pack One's meeting was nearly over by the time David and Goliath arrived.

William's idea was that if Pack One did have the medal they wouldn't be able to resist showing it off on their badge. He intended to be there to claim it back.

David and Goliath's job was to provide a diversion.

It was easy enough. Goliath was a diversion all by himself, and all the Pack One cubs crowded round making a fuss over him.

Pack One's Cub Master was a teacher called Miss Hollings, who also happened to be David's social studies teacher.

She looked surprised but quite pleased to see him. "Thinking of joining us, David?"

"Well, maybe," said David, keeping his fingers crossed behind his back. "Can I just watch for awhile?"

He tried very hard *not* to look at the uniformed figure slipping into the gym and mingling with the other Cubs.

"Certainly," said Miss Hollings graciously. "We're just about to have our Best Den award. Gather round, Pack!"

The Pack formed up and Miss Hollings peered at her notes through her glasses. "This week the winner is— Den Six!"

The denner from Den Six stepped forward, looking very proud. Miss Hollings turned to the cupboard behind her—then turned back, looking at her Pack.

"Just one moment—something very odd is going on."

Everybody turned and stared at William, who was trying not to be noticed at the end of the line!

"It's a spy!" someone shouted. "A spy from the B Team. Get him!"

William disappeared underneath a pile of angry Cubs.

"Wait, listen!" shouted David and went to help.

It wasn't a good idea. All the Cubs who hadn't already jumped on William jumped on *him!*

Goliath, who thought it was all a

splendid game, jumped on top of everyone, barking furiously.

The gym was suddenly filled with a pile of wildly struggling Cubs and one

very excited dog, with William and David somewhere underneath.

Suddenly a piercing whistle-blast rang out.

"Stop this disgraceful behavior at once," shouted Miss Hollings. "Is this a Cub Pack or a troop of Banderlog?"

Everybody froze—even Goliath.

"Pack, line up," ordered Miss Hollings. "William and David, out here in front!"

When the now distinctly rumpled-looking Pack was lined up, Miss Hollings turned to David and William. "Well?"

William drew a deep breath. "Well, it was like this." He explained his idea, about Pack Number One taking the medal for a joke.

When he'd finished Miss Hollings said, "I see. Well, I have to admit, there

are one or two bright sparks here who
might think that sort of thing was
funny." She took a badge from the
cupboard. "But as you can see, we've
only our own badge here." She turned
to the Pack. "Does anyone here know
anything about the missing medal?"

"No, Cub Master," chanted the Pack, speaking like one Cub.

"Cubs' honor?" demanded Miss Hollings sternly.

"Cubs' honor."

She turned to William. "I hope that puts your mind at rest?"

William gulped and said bravely, "Yes, Akela. And I'd like to say sorry to your Pack for suspecting them . . ."

"Never mind, William," said David when they were outside. "It was still a good idea—and even their Cub Master admitted they *might* have thought of it just for fun."

"I was wrong, though," said William. "It's up to you and Goliath now."

Rather sadly William went off home and David lingered for a while outside the gym.

He turned to Goliath. "You were there, you must have seen what happened. If only you could tell me!"

Goliath looked hard at him for a moment, then raised his head to the sky and barked loudly several times.

It was almost as if he was trying to tell David something.

David looked up too—and suddenly saw the answer . . .

All he had to do now was prove it.

Chapter Four

The Master Criminal Returns

David's behavior puzzled everyone that weekend.

On Saturday morning he set off carrying a knapsack full of equipment and supplies, leaving a puzzled Goliath behind.

He didn't get back until just before dark.

On Sunday he did the same thing.

On Sunday evening he got back even
later, looking tired but happy.

On Monday he went to see Mr.
Rogers, Pack Two's Cub Master, and
they had a long private talk . . .

It was Cub Night for Pack Two, and
once again David and Goliath were
there as visitors.

When the time came for the Best Den award, Mr. Rogers paraded the Pack and made a special announcement.

"Now, you all know what happened last week—but you don't all know what's been happening since. Our friend David here has been working very hard on investigating the mystery. I won't tell you yet what he's discovered. Instead, we're going to repeat last week's ceremony and see what happens . . ."

Their Cub Master looked at his notebook.

Then, just as before, he said, "This week, the winner of the badge and medal is . . . Den Six!"

Just as before, William stepped forward.

Just as before, Mr. Rogers said, "Well done, Den Six!" He turned to the cupboard, took down the badge from the top shelf and said, "It gives me great pleasure . . ."

He held out the badge—and suddenly it wasn't just like before any more.

There, hanging from its peg in the middle of the badge, was the gleaming B-P medal!

A huge cheer went up from the Pack, and everybody crowded around David asking for explanations.

"What happened?" demanded William.

"Where did you find it?" asked Peter.

"Who? How? When? Where? Why?" the rest of the Pack wanted to know.

Goliath barked excitedly, and David stroked his head. "Well, old Goliath here gave me the clue . . ."

Suddenly David broke off and turned his head toward the roof. "If you'll all do as I say for a few minutes, I may be able to do better than just tell you what happened. Maybe I can show you . . . It's just possible the master criminal is about to strike again!"

"Go right ahead, David," said the Cub Master. "You've done pretty well so far."

Still whispering, David said, "What I

want you all to do, is spread out along the sides of the gym and keep absolutely quiet. William, you take Goliath with you. Keep whispering 'Hush!' in his ear. Can I have the badge, please, sir?"

Mr. Rogers handed David the badge. He and the rest of the Pack crept to the sides of the gym, lining the walls like statues.

David stood on a chair, put the badge back on the top shelf, then got down quietly and stood there in absolute silence.

Suddenly they heard a light pattering sound on the roof.

A dark shape swooped through the high open window and landed on top of the cupboard.

It was a bright blue bird with a jaunty crest on the top of its head.

It stood, head cocked and bright eyes gleaming wickedly, looking around the gym.

No one moved.

The bird left the cupboard, hovered for a moment, then landed again on the top shelf. It pecked for a moment at the bright spot in the middle of the shelf, then took off again, something bright and silvery gleaming in its beak.

"Hey stop!" yelled William, rushing forward, but it was far too late.

The blue jay fluttered through the

open window and disappeared. William turned to David. "Well, you found the thief all right—but you've just let him pinch the medal again!"

"No I haven't," said David cheerfully. He held out his hand, and there was the medal. "All the blue jay got away with was a soda-bottle top, he'll be just as happy with that!"

Over a celebration feast of orange juice and doughnuts, David explained.

"I was just as baffled as anyone else— until I asked Goliath and he barked at the sky! I looked up and saw the blue jay on the roof. I'd heard stories about blue jays stealing anything shiny, so I realized at once what must have happened. The blue jay flew in while we were all outside, saw the polished medal gleaming in the sunlight and pinched it!" David took a drink of orange juice. "The hard part was finding his nest. I spent all weekend hiding in the bushes, watching the blue jays through binoculars, and finally managed to track down the right tree. I told Cub Master on Monday, and we borrowed one of the caretaker's

ladders, found the nest—and there was the medal! The blue jay was pretty cross when we took it, so I'm not surprised he decided to try again!"

"We'll just keep that cupboard door shut in the future," said Mr. Rogers. He handed William the badge. "There you are—and look out for dive-bombing blue jays on the way home."

William said, "I think David really ought to have it."

"I can't," said David. "I'm not a Cub Scout!"

"Not yet," said William. "But you soon will be, won't you?"

David grinned. "This seems to be where we came in!"

"We'd be pleased to have you, David," said Mr. Rogers.

"That's right," said William. "And

Goliath can be the Pack mascot!"

He tossed Goliath the remains of his doughnut, and Goliath snapped it up and barked for more.

"There you are," said William. "Goliath agrees!"

David ruffled the fur on Goliath's shaggy head. "Well, Goliath usually gets what he wants! How soon can I join?"

More Fun, Mystery, And Adventure With Goliath–

Goliath And The Burglar
The first Goliath story tells how David persuades his parents to buy him a puppy. When Goliath grows very big it appears that he might have to leave the household. David is worried—until a burglar enters the house, and Goliath becomes a hero! (Paperback, ISBN 3820-7—Library Binding, ISBN 5823-2)

Goliath And The Buried Treasure
When Goliath discovers how much fun it is to dig holes, both he and David get into trouble with the neighbors. Meanwhile, building developers have plans that will destroy the city park—until Goliath's skill at digging transforms him into the most unlikely hero in town! (Paperback, ISBN 3819-3—Library Binding, ISBN 5822-4)

Goliath On Vacation
David persuades his parents to bring Goliath with them on vacation—but the big hound quickly disrupts life at the hotel. Goliath is in trouble with David's parents, but he soon redeems himself when he helps David solve the mystery of the disappearing ponies. (Paperback, ISBN 3821-5—Library Binding, ISBN 5824-0)

Goliath At The Dog Show
Goliath helps David solve the mystery at the dog show—then gets a special prize for his effort! (Paperback, ISBN 3818-5—Library Binding, ISBN 5821-6)

Goliath's Christmas
Goliath plays a big part in rescuing a snowstorm victim. Then he and David join friends for the best Christmas party ever. (Paperback, ISBN 3878-9—Library Binding, ISBN 5843-7)

Goliath's Easter Parade
With important help from Goliath, David finds a way to save the neighborhood playground by raising funds at the Easter Parade. (Paperback, ISBN 3957-2—Library Binding, ISBN 5877-1)

Written by Terrance Dicks and illustrated by Valerie Littlewood, all Goliath books at bookstores. Or order direct from Barron's. Paperbacks $2.95 each, Library Bindings $7.95 each. When ordering direct from Barron's, please indicate ISBN number and add 10% postage and handling (Minimum $1.75). N.Y. residents add sales tax. ISBN Prefix: 0-8120

250 Wireless Boulevard, Hauppauge, NY 11788
Call toll free: 1-800-645-3476, in NY 1-800-257-5729